Summer Wonders

by Bob Raczka   illustrated by Judy Stead

www.av2books.com

Your AV² Media Enhanced book gives you a fiction readalong online. Log on to www.av2books.com and enter the unique book code from this page to use your readalong.

AV² Readalong Navigation

Go to **www.av2books.com**, and enter this book's unique code.

BOOK CODE

L365049

AV² by Weigl brings you media enhanced books that support active learning.

First Published by

ALBERT WHITMAN & COMPANY
Publishing children's books since 1919

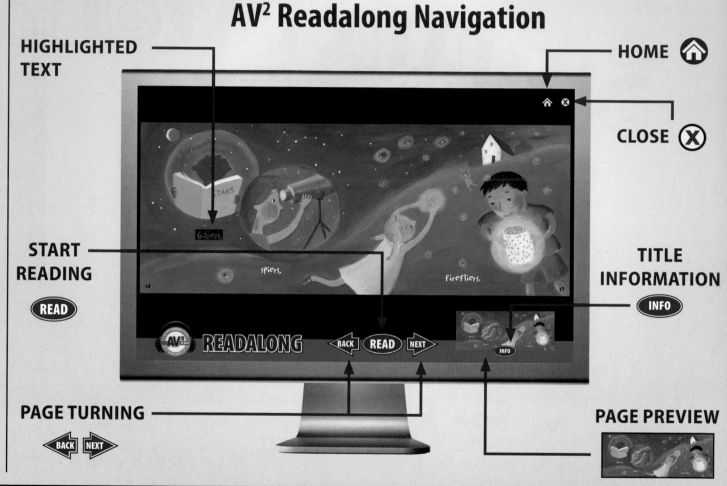

HIGHLIGHTED TEXT

HOME 🏠

CLOSE ⊗

START READING

READ

TITLE INFORMATION

INFO

PAGE TURNING

PAGE PREVIEW

Published by AV² by Weigl
350 5ᵗʰ Avenue, 59ᵗʰ Floor New York, NY 10118
Copyright ©2013 AV² by Weigl
Printed in the United States of America in North Mankato, Minnesota
1 2 3 4 5 6 7 8 9 0   16 15 14 13 12

Text copyright © 2009 by Bob Raczka.
Illustrations copyright © 2009 by Judy Stead.
Published in 2009 by Albert Whitman & Company.

052012
WEP160512

Library of Congress Cataloging-in-Publication Data

Raczka, Bob.
 Summer wonders / by Bob Raczka ; illustrated by Judy Stead.
   p. cm.
 Summary: Illustrations and rhyming text celebrate the sights and sounds of summer, from days of diving and swimming to nights of stargazing and fireflies.
 ISBN 978-1-61913-125-5 (hardcover : alk. paper)
 [1. Stories in rhyme. 2. Summer--Fiction.] I. Stead, Judy, ill. II. Title.
 PZ8.3.R1155Sum 2012
 [E]--dc23
                    2012021486

To Carl, my middle guy, who was born in July.—B.R.

To Marguerite Greer, with love and memories of
sunny summer days at Long Beach.—J.S.

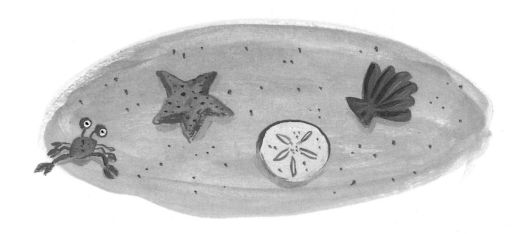

Divers,

swimmers,

5

6

flat rock skimmers.

7

Joggers,

walkers,

sidewalk chalkers.

9

Marchers,

pipers,

12

stars and stripers.

13

Sliders,

swingers,

picnic bringers.

Readers,

rhymers,

tall-tree climbers.

19

Growers,   weeders,

melon eaters.

Fanners,

sippers,

22

ice cream drippers.

Combers,

rakers,

26

castle makers.

STARS

Gazers,

spiers,

28

firefliers.

29

Summer.

Mini Ice Pops

Did you know the first ice pop was invented almost one hundred years ago by an eleven-year-old boy? It happened by accident. Frank Epperson left his fruit-flavored soda outside with a stirring stick in it, and it froze that way. He called his invention the "Epsicle Ice Pop."

You can make your own Mini Ice Pops. They're easy, they're fun, and you can make any flavor you like.

Here's what you'll need:
- An empty ice-cube tray
- A box of toothpicks (flat ones work best)
- Plastic wrap
- A pitcher of fruit juice or your favorite powdered drink

1. With help from Mom or Dad, carefully fill a clean ice-cube tray with your favorite fruit drink.

2. Cover the ice-cube tray tightly with plastic wrap.

3. Stick a toothpick through the plastic wrap and into the center of each juice-filled "cup."

4. Put the ice-cube tray in the freezer.

5. Wait 2 to 3 hours, or until the juice is frozen.

When the juice is completely frozen, ask Mom or Dad to twist the tray to release the Mini Ice Pops. Then hold them by the toothpicks and slurp away!

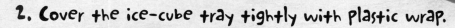

The best part is, you'll have plenty to share with your friends!

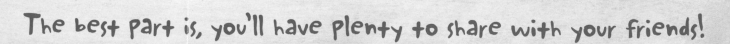